mary-kateandashley

TWO of a kind™

Diaries

Making a Splash

Look for more

TWO of a kind ™

titles:

mary-kateandashley

TWO of a kind™
Diaries
Making a Splash

by Megan Stine

from the series created by Robert Griffard
& Howard Adler

HarperCollins*Entertainment*
An Imprint of HarperCollins*Publishers*

A PARACHUTE PRESS BOOK

A PARACHUTE PRESS BOOK

Parachute Publishing, L.L.C.
156 Fifth Avenue
Suite 325
New York, NY 10010

First published in the USA by Harper Entertainment 2003
First published in Great Britain by HarperCollins*Entertainment* 2004
HarperCollins*Entertainment* is an imprint of HarperCollins*Publishers* Ltd,
77-85 Fulham Palace Road, Hammersmith, London, W6 8JB

The HarperCollins children's website address is
www.harpercollinschildrensbooks.co.uk

2

ISBN 0 00 715886 6

Printed and bound in Great Britian by Clays Ltd, St Ives plc

Chapter 1

Sunday

Dear Diary,

Today was one of the best – and the  worst – days I've had since I came to Camp Evergreen. Right now I'm so tired, I don't even know where to begin! I'm lying on my bunk in the Tree Frogs cabin. The lights are all out, and everyone else is asleep. But you know me, Diary. I've got a flashlight under the covers!

I guess I'll start with the good news first. I've been hanging out with the coolest and most fun people at camp – my cabin mates: Allison, Claire, Mindy, Emily and my twin sister, Ashley.

Allison is the noisiest one of the bunch – but only because she sneezes all the time! She's allergic to everything! Claire is a born leader and is super-brainy. She's tall, with short brown hair and glasses. Mindy is sort of Claire's opposite. Not so tall, with long wavy dark hair. She has tons of tie-dyed shirts and is *way* into astrology. Emily is shy and was homesick at first, but I think Ashley is pulling her out of her shell a little.

Some of the guys are tons of fun to be with, too – especially Patrick. I think he has a crush on me! Me,

Ash and our Evergreen friends make an awesome team. We've all been working to beat Ravenwood, the enemy camp down the road.

The rivalry between the two camps goes way back, Diary. A long time ago two sisters founded a summer camp. They called it Camp McArdle

because that was their last name. But then the sisters had a big fight, and they split the camp into two smaller ones. Each summer since, there have been tons of contests to see which camp is best. So far we're losing in the official intercamp competition to Ravenwood.

But there's another challenge – a secret one that both camps really want to win. It's one of the coolest things about Camp Evergreen!

We heard about it from our counsellor, Jill, the first day we were here. She told us that when the McArdle sisters were alive, they had a portrait of themselves painted and they hung it up at their camp. But after the argument, only one camp could have the portrait – and Camp Evergreen got it. But the next summer the campers from Ravenwood stole it. And then Evergreen stole it back!

Years later it became a tradition for one camp to try to take the portrait from the other. Whoever has it at the end of the summer wins the secret challenge!

Well, guess what? Today we did it. We stole the Founders' Portrait from those creeps over at Ravenwood!

We took it to the Evergreen main lodge, where we eat our meals and we have meetings and stuff. Then we hung it over the fireplace. We figured the Ravenwood kids would try to get the portrait back, so we decided to spend the night in the lodge to guard it.

We were so psyched when we went back to our cabin to get our sleeping bags. That's when the bad part of my day started.

I found a note on my bunk. It was from Jessie, my camp Little Sister. She's only seven years old. The note said she had run away!

My heart started thumping, Diary. Because deep down I knew Jessie had run away because I yelled at her. I couldn't help it. Jessie had tattled on Ashley and got her in big trouble.

I know I shouldn't have lost my temper. I was supposed to be looking out for her, not scolding her!

I ran to Jessie's cabin to see if she was there. I was hoping that maybe the note was a joke. But it wasn't. She was gone!

Lisa, the counsellor in Jessie's cabin, jumped up when she realised what had happened. "I'll go wake Nancy," Lisa said. Nancy is the director of Camp Evergreen. "You go to bed."

I didn't say anything. I headed back to my cabin, but I wasn't going to bed. I wanted to find Jessie. And I had an idea where she might be.

I grabbed my flashlight, then headed towards the woods. The wind blew through the trees, making them moan. A shiver crawled up my spine. Calm down, I told myself. If you're spooked, just imagine what Jessie is feeling!

"Jessie," I called. "Where are you?" Only the wind answered.

I wanted to run back to my bunk but I kept going. "Jessie, please answer me!"

Then I heard it – a rustling sound. I knew it was probably just a raccoon but I went towards it.

I heard it again. The sound was coming from a tree. I ran up to it and shone my flashlight into the hollow in its trunk. There she was! Curled up inside with a scowl on her little face.

"Jessie!" I cried. "Are you okay? Come out of there."

"No," she said. "I'm staying right here."

"You can't," I said. "Nancy and Lisa are both really worried about you. I've been worried too."

"So what? They don't like me. You don't like me. No one likes me."

"Oh, Jessie, I like you. I think you're great." I knelt in front of her and took her hands. "And I didn't mean to yell at you."

"Really?" She looked up at me doubtfully.

I nodded. "And I'll never do it again. I promise. But you have to promise *me* that you'll never run away again."

"I guess," Jessie said reluctantly. Then she smiled. "I'm hungry, Mary-Kate. Can we get a peanut butter and banana sandwich?" Her eyes were sparkling and she was smiling, so I knew we were friends again. I took her hand and helped her out of the hollow tree. We walked back through the woods to the main part of camp. I took Jessie back to her cabin, where Jill promised to give Nancy the good news.

On the way, I thought about how proud I was of being Jessie's Big Sister. And how much I loved camp. I never wanted to leave!

Then I remembered what my bunk mate, Claire, had said. "Why don't you become a C.I.T., a counsellor in training. Then you can keep coming back!"

That's not a bad idea, now that I think about it. I mean, why not? The C.I.T.s have a lot of fun. They get to stay up late every night and sleep in their own cabin – with no older counsellor. And they get to have a huge cool party at the end of the summer.

Okay, I decided right then and there. I'm going to be a C.I.T. next year. I'm going to talk to Nancy about it as soon as I can.

I'll let you know what happens, Diary!

It's the next morning, Diary, and I just came back from talking to Nancy. I found her in the lodge office and knocked on her door.

"Hi," I said. "Nancy, can I ask you something?"

"Oh, hello, Mary-Kate," she said. "Sure, come in. I was just going to come and find you."

"You were?" My eyes opened wide. "How come?"

"Well, I wanted to thank you for finding Jessie last night," Nancy said. "And there's something else. But you go first. What did you want to ask me?"

I cleared my throat, trying to sound responsible. "I was thinking about being a C.I.T. next year," I said. "And I wanted to know what to do to get the job."

Nancy's face grew serious. "Oh, I don't know about that, Mary-Kate," she said. "I'm not sure you're ready."

"How come?" I was so surprised. "You just said I did a good job finding Jessie."

"Yes," Nancy agreed. "But that's what I wanted to tell you. Jessie talked to her parents this morning. She told them why she ran away. Now her parents don't want you to be her Big Sister any more."

"Why not?" I asked even though I knew the answer.

"Right or wrong, they blame you for Jessie running away," Nancy explained. "And the campers' parents need to trust all our counsellors. Even the ones in training have to be responsible."

"They can trust me," I argued. "I'm *totally* responsible!" I couldn't believe she was calling *me* irresponsible. I'm the queen of responsibility back at White Oak, the boarding school Ashley and I go to. "Won't you at least give me a chance to prove it to you?" I asked her.

Nancy nodded. "We'll see."

So now I'm trying to figure out a way to show her I'd make a great C.I.T. – so I can come back to Camp Evergreen next summer.

The only problem is, how?

You see why yesterday was the best – and the worst – day of my whole summer?

Dear Diary,

I have only a few minutes to write this, but I have to tell you how upset I am! I have to go say goodbye to the nicest boy in camp, Andrew Worth. He's going home!

7

I was just talking about it with my friends Claire and Mindy. We were all hanging out in the cabin before breakfast.

"It's not fair," Mindy said. "Andrew is the best tennis player we've got! How can his dad send him home *now*, right before our big tennis match against Ravenwood?"

Claire nodded. "And if that happens, we'll lose the whole intercamp competition!"

"Who cares about that," Mindy said. "What about Ashley?" She gave me a sympathetic look. That's because she knows how much I like Andrew. We've been hanging out all summer and I didn't want him to leave.

Mindy stared intently at an astrology chart. That's her thing. She totally plans her life around the stars. "I don't see it," she said, shaking her head. "Andrew's moon and sun are both in the right place. This should be a good time for him, not a bad one."

"I know. You showed me his chart," I said. "Besides, it's the middle of camp! How can his dad send him home now?"

No one answered me because everyone knew the reason Andrew was leaving. Andrew's dad, Coach Worth, had told

him he wasn't allowed to hang out with me. His dad said being with girls took his mind off tennis. Then the coach found out we'd been spending time together anyway. And *ka-boom!* Coach Worth exploded.

So today is Andrew's last day. That's why I've got to run. I have to say good-bye before he leaves!

I'll finish this when I get back.

Okay, I'm back. And you'll never believe what happened! I walked over to Andrew's cabin and knocked on the door. He was sitting inside, on his bunk. "Hi," he said.

I glanced around, wondering why he wasn't packed up. "I came to say goodbye," I said, sitting on his bed.

"Thanks," Andrew nodded. "That's so nice. I was going to come say bye to *you*. But I decided not to."

"How come?" I asked, swallowing hard. Didn't he care that I was going to miss him? Wasn't he going to miss *me*?

A little grin crept into the corners of Andrew's mouth. "Because I'm not leaving!" he announced, and the grin spread into a huge smile.

"That's awesome!" I cried. On an impulse I jumped up and hugged him. "I can't believe it!"

"I talked to my dad," Andrew said really fast. "I

told him it just wasn't fair for him to decide how I spend all my time."

"Right!" I said, totally agreeing. "But did he buy that?" I couldn't quite picture it. Coach Worth had been pretty tough on everyone on the tennis team – *especially* Andrew. He thought Andrew had the potential to be a professional player.

"Not at first," Andrew admitted. "But I said I'd quit playing tennis completely if he kept pushing me so hard."

"Wow," I said. "But you love tennis. I didn't think you'd want to give it up."

"I don't. It was a gamble," Andrew said, shrugging, "and it worked. My dad agreed to let me stay. I can do whatever I want in my free time – as long as I still stick to my practice schedule."

"Cool!" I said, slapping him five.

"Nice serve," Andrew joked. "Just put a little more power into it."

I laughed and we slapped five again. This time he squeezed my hand. I felt a little shiver all over. Every time he touched my hand, it made me feel like melted butter inside.

"Oh! And guess what else? My friend, Brooke, is coming to camp this morning!" Andrew announced. "She and Max and I have been hanging out here every summer for five years. You're going to love her."

I knew Max. He was a great guy, but I hadn't heard about Brooke until now.

"How come she's coming to camp so late?" I asked.

"Her parents took her to Europe," Andrew said. "I can't wait for you to meet her. I think she's going to be in your cabin."

"That's cool," I said. "What's she like?"

"Oh, she's the best," Andrew said. "She's funny and smart. Every year we go wild playing pranks around camp. We're always daring each other to do crazy stuff."

Yeah. I could picture that. Andrew and Max were big pranksters. Their sneakiness was a major reason we stole back the portrait last night.

"Hey," Andrew said, checking his watch. "Breakfast is in five minutes. Want to eat together?"

"Sure," I said. "I'll meet you in the mess hall in sixty seconds." Then I ran back here to finish writing this, Diary.

Isn't it the best news? Andrew gets to stay, and his friend Brooke will be arriving here any minute!

I can't wait to meet her. If she's as much fun as Andrew says, this summer is going to be a blast!

Chapter 2

Monday

Dear Diary,

Andrew was right. Brooke *is* going to be bunking with the Tree Frogs. So, we all thought it would be cool to be in  the cabin when she arrives. Well, most of us are here. Allison had an early practice for the big tennis

match against Ravenwood this afternoon. Poor thing had to stuff a wad of tissues in her pocket. She says her allergies are the worst in the morning. I'm in the tennis tournament, too, but I've been practising so hard that the coach told me to rest. I guess I'm as ready as I'll ever be!

Anyway, I hope Brooke gets here soon. Mindy, Emily, Mary-Kate and I are sitting on Emily's bunk, checking out her prize scrapbook.

Emily misses her family and friends a lot, and her scrapbook is the one thing that lifts her spirits. And it's awesome! A real work of art, with heavy pink and purple paper, covered with pictures from home – her cat, her room, her friends. Plus there are cute notes from her classmates, lots of pressed flowers, and all kinds of drawings.

"Hey, Claire," I said. "Stop

organising your T-shirts and take a look at this!"

"What?" Claire asked. She placed her perfectly folded Camp Evergreen shirt into her footlocker and sat next to me.

"This is so cool!" Mindy said, turning the pages of Emily's book.

"It's the best scrapbook I've ever seen," I agreed. "I wish I had the patience to make one for myself."

Emily smiled but didn't say anything. She's still pretty shy, even after three weeks of camp.

"You should make a scrapbook about the Camp Evergreen and Ravenwood competitions," Mary-Kate said.

"Not unless we win," Claire added. "And we're losing right now. Who wants a scrapbook about being a loser?"

"Not me," a voice said from the screen door. A tall and tan girl was standing outside. She had long blonde hair – longer than mine – but she wore it pulled back in a ponytail. She was wearing a black tank top and black shorts. Her arms were full with a duffel bag, towels, a tote bag and a tennis racquet. "Can I come in?" she asked, shrugging so that someone would get the door.

Claire leaped to open it for her. "Are you Brooke?"

"Yes, and please don't kill me for bringing so much stuff!" Brooke said. "I know there's room for only six girls in Tree Frogs. But Nancy said this was the best place for me. They're going to bring a rollaway cot and stick it over there somewhere." She pointed to the corner next to my bed.

"Hey, you'll be right near me!" I said.

"Cool!" Brooke smiled. "What's your name?"

"Ashley," I replied.

Brooke raised her eyebrows. "Oh, so *you're* Ashley," she said with a devilish grin. "Andrew told me about you."

"Really?" I said, not that I was surprised. I mean, of course Andrew would have told Brooke about me. He and I have been seeing each other since the first week at camp. But it was the *way* Brooke said it that made me curious. "What did he say?"

"Oh, nothing much," Brooke said, dropping her stuff with a sigh. "He just wrote me about you a few times." Then she turned away to the others and said, "I am so glad to be back at Evergreen. So, how are we going to kick off the rest of the summer?"

"I'm Mindy. And you're a Sagittarius, right, Brooke?" Mindy asked.

Brooke's eyes opened wide. "Totally right!" she said. "So I guess no one bothers to hide their diaries from Mindy! She already knows what's going on!"

We all laughed, and then everyone else introduced themselves.

"Hey, I've got an idea," Brooke said. "Why don't we each tell a secret that we've never told *anyone?* That way we'll get to know each other."

"Only if you go first," Emily said.

Wow, I thought. That was bold of Emily. She obviously didn't want to tell Brooke a secret. And I wasn't so sure I did, either. I hardly knew the girl.

"Okay," Brooke said. "I've never told anyone how I get the softest pillow in this whole camp – every single year!" She leaned in close to the people around her and whispered something.

Claire, Emily, Mindy and Mary-Kate all laughed.

"Hold on. I missed that, Brooke," I said.

"So now it's your turn," Brooke said to Mindy.

Wait a minute. Did she just ignore me? I glanced at Mary-Kate, but she didn't seem to notice. Maybe Brooke didn't hear me, I decided.

"Hmmm," Mindy said. "A secret I've never told anyone. . . I can't think of anything."

"*I'll* tell you a secret," Claire offered. "We're going to miss morning swim if we sit around here all day!"

Typical Claire. She likes to stay on a schedule.

"Okay," Brooke agreed. "But before the day is over, Mindy and everyone else has to come up with a secret."

"I'll try," Mindy agreed as we left the cabin.

"So, Brooke, what activities are you signing up for?" I asked as we crossed the camp.

Brooke turned to Claire. "So did you guys know there's a way to get extra desserts from the cooks?"

Brooke didn't hear me *that* time, either? I didn't think so. I was standing right next to her!

I pulled Mary-Kate aside. "Did you just see that?" I whispered. "Brooke totally ignored me."

"Come on, Ashley, why would she do that?" Mary-Kate said. "She just met you. And she seems like so much fun!"

Right. Okay. She's fun. Andrew said I'd have a great time hanging out with her. So why did I have such a bad feeling about this girl?

Dear Diary,

The day started off perfectly. We met our new bunk mate, Brooke, who's totally cool. Then after morning swim, I went canoeing. We were supposed to meet by the

big old iron anchor that sits on the shore near the boathouse. And when I got there, I found out that Patrick had signed up to canoe, too.

"Hey, want to be boat buddies?" he asked me.

16

There's no need to tell you how I answered, right, Diary? I mean, come on. Patrick is so smart and nice. And he's really cute, too. Who *wouldn't* want to be his partner?

It was just the two of us in one canoe. We paddled out to the middle of the lake. Then he started making us go in circles.

"Don't paddle on the same side I'm paddling on!" I said.

"Why not?" Patrick asked.

"Because we'll be out here all day!" I said, laughing. I knew he was doing it to be funny.

"I know," he said. "I can deal with staying out here all day. *Canoe?*"

I turned around to see him giving me a goofy grin. "That's so lame," I said, but I couldn't help laughing at the joke.

"I know, but I can make even lamer jokes. . . *canoe?*" he said.

I don't know why I laughed again. From anyone else, the joke would be too corny. But coming from him, it was cute.

Anyway, we both finally got hungry, and we paddled back to shore just in time for lunch. We slid our canoe on the sand by the anchor and took the fastest path to the lodge.

I took in a deep breath of fresh air. The day was

perfect. Not too hot, not too cool. I was so glad that my dad had suggested Ashley and I come to Camp Evergreen. It was the camp that he went to as a boy. Why hadn't we come here sooner? I wondered. One year was not enough. Well, hopefully I'd get to come back as a C.I.T. next summer.

"Evergreen is so awesome," I said, staring at the beautiful trees surrounding us.

"I know," Patrick agreed. "I love it here. That's why I applied to be a C.I.T. next year."

"You're kidding," I said. "Me, too!" Even more reason to want to come back to camp, Diary. There has to be a way to convince Nancy I was right for the job.

When we reached the dining hall, Patrick went to eat with his bunk mates. "See you at the campfire tonight, Mary-Kate."

"Okay," I told him. We had a campfire every night at Evergreen. I spotted Ashley, and the two of us grabbed plates full of salad and fried fish.

"Our usual table is full," Ashley said. So, we sat at the only open table, where some of the counsellors were eating. And I'm so glad we did.

"I'm stuck," one of the counsellors was saying. His name was Rick. "John got the flu, so he's in the infirmary."

18

Making A Splash

I knew John Fisker. He was one of the C.I.T.s.

"Whoa," Jill said. She was the Tree Frog's counsellor. "You've got that whole cabin full of seven-year-old boys – and no C.I.T. to help?"

Rick nodded.

"That's ugly," Jill said, shaking her head.

"What are you going to do? That cabin is the worst," another counsellor asked.

"I'll help!" I cried from my end of the table before Rick could answer.

Rick laughed. "I wish," he said.

"No, really. I want to be a C.I.T. next year," I said. "I could help you until John gets better."

Rick glanced at Jill. She sort of nodded.

"Well, okay," he said with a shrug. "But you'll have to ask Nancy first."

Yes! This was my big chance! Right after lunch I hurried to Nancy's office and told her my plan.

"I don't know, Mary-Kate," she said. "A junior counsellor has a lot of responsibilities. You have to be able to handle more than one child at a time. And you can't lose your temper."

"I've learned from my mistakes. I *know* I can do this!" I wanted to sound as convincing as possible, so I added, "And Rick, the regular counsellor, will always be nearby, right? If I have a problem, he can help."

"But what about your own camp activities?" Nancy said. "You should be here to learn new things and have fun."

"I'll do *both*," I said. "This way I can prove to you that I'm responsible enough to be a C.I.T. next year."

Nancy glanced at me for a minute. I couldn't tell what she was thinking, but I figured I might have scored some points.

Finally she nodded and smiled. "All right. I'll give you a try, but for only part of each day. And only until John gets better."

"Thank you!" I was so happy, I wanted to hug her. But I didn't.

"You can start now," Nancy said. "The younger children have a rest period. Rick is over in the Toadstool cabin. Go see what he wants you to do."

"I'm there," I said. Then I hurried over to meet the boys.

But as I neared the Toadstool cabin, I heard yelling and screaming and thumping and jumping inside. What were they *doing* in there? I stepped through the door and a pillow flew straight at me, just missing my head.

"Whoa!" I said, catching the pillow. "What's up?"

The boys were having an all-out pillow fight. Four of them were standing on their bunks, hurling pillows. Two more were crouched on the floor, throwing balled-up shirts from below.

"Where's Rick?" I asked as one of the boys thwapped another with a shirt.

"Bathroom," a red-haired kid said.

"Well, I'm Mary-Kate," I said loudly, trying to sound as if I were in charge. "I'm going to take over for John until he gets better."

"John was teaching us how to juggle," the red-haired one said. "Can you juggle?"

Juggle? "No," I started to say. But before I even got out the word, another boy threw a sopping wet sponge at me.

"Juggle this!" he shouted.

I ducked. "Hey! Stop that! We need to settle down. Why don't you guys tell me your names?"

"No way!" a boy with a wild crop of curly black hair said. "We don't like girls!"

"But you'll like me. Really," I said and turned to the redhead. "Come on. What's your name?"

"Ethan," he said, still standing on a bunk. He started jumping up and down, yelling his name over and over. "Ethan, Ethan, Ethan!"

"Okay! How about the rest of you?" I asked.

None of the others spoke, so Ethan did. "That's Ben," he said, nodding to a boy whose two front teeth were missing. "And he's Mojo." He pointed to the kid with the curly hair.

"I'm David," a little blond kid said with a grin.

"Good!" I said, trying to memorise the names. I turned to the last two. "How about you guys?"

"David," one of the last two said, and all the others burst out laughing.

Something told me he was lying, but I decided to ignore him. I turned to the last kid – the one with the big ears. "Well?" I asked him.

"David," he said, sputtering a laugh.

 Three Davids in one cabin? I didn't think so.

"Get her!" the biggest David yelled. "She's the enemy!"

All six of them threw pillows and shirts at me.

Oh, no! I thought as I ducked for cover. What have I got myself into? But then I grabbed a pillow and took aim. After all, no one likes a good pillow fight more than me!

Besides, Mary-Kate Burke is not a quitter!

Chapter 3

Monday

Dear Diary,

This afternoon was the last round of
the tennis tournament between Camp
Evergreen and Camp Ravenwood.
Andrew won his match and all the Evergreen
campers cheered. It seemed as if Brooke was shouting the loudest. Nobody can say she's not a good
friend to Andrew. She was sitting in the crowded
stands with Mary-Kate, Emily and Mindy.

Too bad Allison lost *her* match right after that.

"Camp Ravenwood is still ahead in the points,"
Coach Worth said. "So it's up to you, Ashley."

Talk about pressure. If I lost this match, not only
would we lose the tennis tournament against Ravenwood, we'd lose the whole intercamp competition!

"Come on, Ashley. You can do it!" Andrew yelled
from the sidelines.

All my friends were clap-
ping and shouting out my
name. But when I looked up
into the stands, I noticed that
Brooke wasn't. In fact, she was
reading a fashion magazine.

Not very nice, if you ask me. But I couldn't think
about her. I needed to stay focused on the game.

23

And I did. And guess what, Diary?

"We won!" I cried after my final serve of the game. The Ravenwood girl was too slow and she missed it!

The Evergreen kids raced off the stands and swarmed the court.

"We're the champs!" I cheered, jumping up and down. Andrew rushed over to me. He grabbed me and twirled me around. "We're the champs!" I cried again, so happy.

I mean, I *thought* that was true. I *thought* I'd just won the game – and the whole competition – against Ravenwood.

Then Coach Worth punched a hole in our happiness balloon. "I'm sorry to say this," he announced after the campers had settled down. "But we just added up all the points. We won the tennis match – but we're only tied with Ravenwood in the overall camp competition."

"Tied?" Andrew said. "But I thought if we won tennis, we'd win the whole thing!"

"Me, too," Coach Worth admitted. "But I was wrong. We received only fourteen points for the tennis part of the competition. So, in the overall games, we're tied."

This was unbelievable. In the entire history of

competitions between Evergreen and Ravenwood, there was never a tie!

Mary-Kate nudged Andrew and me. "At least we have the portrait," she said gleefully. "That makes us the *underground* champs, even if we're tied in the regular competition!"

True, I thought. Not a bad consolation prize.

"And Ashley played the greatest game of her life," Andrew said. "I'm totally proud." He gave me a sweet kiss on the cheek. "Let's do something right now to celebrate. What'll it be?"

Before I could answer, Brooke came running down to us on the court.

"Brooke!" Andrew cried when he saw her. The two of them slapped at each other's hands and did some kind of funky handshake.

"Way to go, Worthless!" she told him.

"Worthless? He's the best thing we have on the team!" I corrected her.

Brooke laughed and tossed her hair over her shoulder. "Relax, Ashton."

"Ash*ley*," I muttered, liking this girl less and less every second I spent with her. How was I supposed to bunk with her for the rest of the summer?

"Worthless is Brooke's nickname for me," Andrew explained, "because my last name is Worth." He turned to her, grinning. "So, hey! How have you been?"

"Great, now that I'm back here at camp!" she said. "Europe was cool, but I kept thinking about you and Max."

As if on cue, Max ran up to join us. He was wearing a sun visor and T-shirt backwards. It was Max's idea of a wild and crazy style. "Wow," he said, staring at Brooke. "You look hot!"

I could tell that he was surprised to see her looking so good. I got the feeling she'd grown up a lot since he saw her last year.

Then Max slapped me five and congratulated me on the big win. "You were awesome today, Ash."

"Thanks," I began. "I—"

"I can't wait for the three of us to hang out!" Brooke said, hooking her arms with Andrew's and Max's. "First I want to hear all the gossip. Then I want us to pull some major stunts. I've had a lot of time to think in Europe, and I have a few ideas that will totally top last summer's!"

"You got it!" Andrew said. "Hey, why don't you tell Ashley about what we did to that really strict counsellor?"

"Maybe later," Brooke said, not even glancing at me. "Right now I want to do something fun!" With that, she pulled the two boys right off the tennis court.

"Bye, Ash!" Max said.

"We'll celebrate later," Andrew called. "Okay?"

"Sure," I said. But with Brooke at camp, I didn't think I'd have much to cheer about.

Dear Diary,

So maybe I *do* have something to cheer about. Nancy announced this morning at breakfast that the older  kids at Evergreen and Ravenwood are going to have a treasure hunt!

It's the tiebreaker for the inter-camp competition. Each camp will get a series of clues. Whichever team figures out the clues and finishes the hunt first wins a mystery prize! And their camp wins the competition!

"You'll get the first clue tomorrow," Nancy said.

"Let's form a team to find the treasure," Brooke said at our table. "We'll roam around both camps like a massive detective force or something."

"Sounds good to me," Max said. He and Andrew were eating with their bunk mates at the table behind us. Max leaned back and nudged Brooke's arm, something he'd been doing all morning.

Now, Diary, if Brooke had been nice to me – even for five seconds – I might have wanted to point out that Max is totally flirting with her, since she doesn't seem to get the hint. But she hasn't been, so I didn't.

"Won't we find the treasure faster if we split up?" Claire argued.

"Maybe," Brooke admitted. "But just think how awesome it will look if we stick together – like a band of pirate thieves or something! When the Ravenwood kids see us, they'll just give up."

I wasn't sure about that. "They didn't give up so easily when we were trying to steal the portrait," I said.

"That was *before* I got here!" Brooke laughed.

Most of my bunk mates laughed right along with her. Even Mary-Kate.

"See? I knew you were a Sagittarius!" Mindy said. "You're *so* ready to roll."

I caught a glimpse of the look on Emily's face, which said *I wish she'd roll right out of here!* I guess Emily and I were the only ones who didn't totally love Brooke.

"We should dress alike, too," Mary-Kate said. "We could make T-shirts that say *Tree Frog Treasure Troop* or something."

"Except, when do we have time for *that?*" Claire asked.

"We don't," Brooke admitted. "But I like throwing around ideas."

"That's how we come up with our best pranks," Andrew said from the other table. "Right, Brooke?"

"Yup," she said, swatting him with her straw. "Come here, we need your brain."

"Can't. Got to go." Andrew got up to clear his breakfast tray after that, and I followed him. After all, it was the first chance I'd had to be alone with him since yesterday, when Brooke practically dragged him away.

"You want to work together on the treasure hunt?" I asked.

"You bet," he said. "We've got to get Brooke and Max on our side, too. We'll make a great team."

"Right." I didn't tell him what I was thinking. That we would be an awesome team – if Brooke wasn't such a witch. Instead I said, "But wouldn't it be great if you and I could spend some time alone?"

He smiled. "I was just thinking the same thing," he said. "The only problem is my dad is keeping me to my tennis schedule. How about we meet tomorrow right after dinner?"

"Our spot by the lake?" I asked.

He nodded. "You know the place."

"It's a date." I tossed my milk carton into the rubbish bin.

"More follow-through, Burke!" he said, joking as if he were coaching my tennis swing. He kissed me, and I felt all melty inside.

The rest of the day went pretty well also. While the other Tree Frogs were following Brooke around like little puppies, Emily and I hung out together. We went to a tie-dying class. She made a T-shirt and I made some cool pillow cases to take home.

Pretty soon we were talking about our lives at home. I told Emily how superclose Mary-Kate and I are. And how we both go to boarding school in New Hampshire, and that our dad is a college professor. Emily told me about her five brothers and sisters and about her love of art and kids and how she wants to be a teacher one day.

Diary, I was so glad that Emily and I decided to do our own thing. I really respected her. Even though she was shy, she wasn't a follower. She knows who she is, and that's way cool.

We were heading back to our cabin when Emily started talking about Brooke. "She's just so . . . *big*," Emily was saying. "It's like she always has to be the center of attention. . . ."

I tried to keep my comments about Brooke to a bare minimum. I didn't want to say anything bad about the girl – even if she wasn't my favourite person. But I have to admit, I did agree with Emily.

Especially when Brooke brushed past us and out of the cabin right then. "Can you believe it?" she said. "I'm here two days and I'm already late for a date with my favorite guys – Andrew and Max."

"Whatever," I muttered, and Emily and I went inside.

Emily decided to take a shower before dinner, and I flopped on my bed to think. *Why is Brooke being so rude to me?* I wondered. *What did I ever do to her? And why do Max and Andrew like her so much?*

I sighed and rolled over to look at the picture of Andrew and me I had pinned on the corkboard above my bed. The one Allison had taken the night Andrew first held my hand.

But it wasn't there. Where was it?

Maybe it slipped off the board and fell behind my bed. I jumped up and looked. It wasn't there, either. And it wasn't under my pillow or in my sheets or in my footlocker.

That's really weird, I thought. *How could something like that just disappear?*

Chapter 4

Wednesday

Dear Diary,

You're never going to believe this one. It all started when I walked into the arts-and-crafts cabin this morning to help Rick with his group of seven-year-old boys.

"Hi, Mary-Kate," Rick said.

"Hi, Marly-Cootie!" Mojo said, cracking up. So did all the other kids.

Marly-Cootie? Where did *that* come from?

"Listen," Rick said. "I've got to run over to the main lodge for a few minutes. Do you think you can handle these guys? You won't be alone. Sarah, the art teacher, is here."

Sarah nodded at me as she laid out strips of leather and beads for the kids.

"Marly-Cootie, Marly-Cootie!" the boys chanted.

"Okay, that's enough," Rick said firmly. "Or we won't climb the big tree after lunch." Instantly the little guys quieted down, and Rick looked at me again. "You feel okay with this?"

"No problem," I said. "Go ahead, we'll be fine."

"Thanks," Rick said.

"Marly-Cootie, can you help me with my beads?" Ethan asked, swiping his red hair out of his eyes.

"Sure." I sat at the table and started stringing.

I can do this! I thought happily. *I wish Nancy could see me now.*

"So, tell me your real names," I said to the three Davids.

"It's David," the blond one said.

"Call me Spider-Man!" another David said.

"He's Rambo!" Ben shouted, pointing at the biggest kid in the group.

"I am not!" the big David yelled back, tossing a bead at Ben. They all started talking and yelling at once.

"Hey – one at a time!" I said, trying to get them quiet.

"Settle down," Sarah added. "Ben – are you making a belt or a necklace?"

"Necklace," Ben said. He picked up a string and hung it on his nose.

"Look! I've got a necklace, too!" Mojo cried, putting a string on *his* nose.

"Boys! We are not playing with the beads that way," Sarah said. "Now, I want you all to get busy. And stay in your seats. This is a quiet project."

So that's the way to handle kids, I thought, watching Sarah. *Just make sure they follow the rules.*

One of the Davids spilled some beads on the floor and Sarah reached down to pick them up.

"Ow!" Sarah cried. She held up her hand. A long wooden splinter was sticking out of her thumb, and blood was flowing down her hand.

"Want me to take it out?" Mojo offered.

Sarah looked pale. "I think I'd better let the nurse do that," she said. "Mary-Kate, will you be okay for a few minutes?"

"Sure," I nodded. Why not? The boys were working quietly. And this was a great chance to prove how responsible I am.

"Thanks," Sarah said. "I'll be right back."

As soon as she was gone, Ben raised his hand. "Marly-Cootie, can you help me?"

I wish they'd stop calling me Marly-Cootie! I thought. But I was determined to get along with them. "What do you need?" I asked.

"Yellow beads," Ben said. "I'm all out."

I stared at the boxes of beads on the table. "I don't think we have any more yellow," I told him. "Sorry, Ben."

"Oh, yes we do," Mojo said. "In there." He pointed to the supply cupboard at the back of the room.

"I'll go take a look," I said. I was happy to help.

Big mistake. I went into the cupboard and turned on the light. "Where are they?" I asked.

Then I heard giggling behind me. And before I could turn around to see what was going on, the door slammed shut! "Hey!" I cried, jiggling the knob. The little monsters had locked me inside!

I pounded on the door for a few minutes, but they wouldn't let me out. All I could do was listen to them laugh. I should have known something like this would happen. For a whole three seconds, this proving-I'm-responsible thing was way too easy!

Dear Diary,

So, I guess that you want to know what happened after the Toadstools locked me in the cupboard. Well, Rick came back a few minutes later and let me out.

"Way to impress me and Nancy," he said.

Can you say "way to totally humiliate yourself, Mary-Kate"? I wondered. *I've got to make sure nothing like this happens again. Or else I'll never be a C.I.T.!*

The only saving grace was that Rick promised not to tell anyone else what happened. Anyway, I'm going to try to put it past me. I still have to have fun at camp, right? That's why I was so psyched when the treasure hunt began. The Toadstools were in swim class that period, so I was free. Rick didn't need me for about two hours.

Nancy and Big Bob, the camp director for Ravenwood, called all the older campers to the Evergreen boathouse on the lake. There were about sixty kids there – thirty from each camp.

Nancy held up two large cardboard keys and explained how the treasure hunt worked. "We have the first clue right here," she said. "It's written on these keys. I'll give one key to each group."

"Here's the deal," Big Bob said. "There are five clues. When you solve the first clue, you'll find two keys with the second clue written on them. Clue number two will lead to clue number three, and so on."

"The clues can be hidden anywhere at either camp," Nancy added. "But we have one important rule. The treasure hunting stops at dinnertime. No searching after dinner. Got that?"

Everyone mumbled yes.

"Okay," Nancy said. "Here's the first clue." She handed one key to the kids from Ravenwood and one to our Evergreen group. "Good luck!"

Making A Splash

It said:

TO FIND THE TREASURE,
THIS CLUE WE WROTE,
WHERE THE NEXT CLUE HIDES,
WON'T FLOAT YOUR BOAT.

"It must be here on the waterfront!" Claire said.

"Let's search the canoes!" Brooke said, taking charge.

All at once, everyone scrambled to search the waterfront. Ashley and Patrick and I looked under every single canoe. Claire and Brooke searched the rowboats and even asked the lifeguard if she'd seen anything. Kids from Ravenwood were doing the same thing. But no one from either camp could find the second clue!

"The word *float* has to mean something," I heard one boy from Ravenwood say.

"Maybe it's on that floating dock in the middle of the lake!" Brooke said, too loudly.

Instantly, the Ravenwood boy dived into the water and swam for the floating dock. Patrick did the same thing. They raced to get there first. But the clue wasn't on the dock either.

"Where could it be?" Ashley wondered out loud.

The Ravenwood kids decided to go back to their

camp to huddle up. And some of the Evergreen kids wandered off, too. That's when Claire and I started reading the clue again.

"It says it *won't* float your boat," Claire muttered. "What doesn't float?"

"Well, that anchor definitely won't float," I said, pointing to the big iron thing that sat near the water's edge.

"That's it!" Claire's eyes lit up and she gripped my arm. Then we both glanced around to make sure no one from Ravenwood was watching.

The coast was clear. So we raced to the anchor. Claire dropped to her knees and looked underneath it. "We rock!" Claire shouted as she held up a black cardboard key with the next clue on it. It read:

> IF YOU DON'T FIND THE NEXT CLUE,
> YOUR TEAM WILL BE TOAST.
> WANT S'MORE HELP?
> TRY THE CAMPFIRE ROAST!

"Campfire?" I pictured the circle of logs where we had campfires almost every night.

"Let's go over to Ravenwood," Claire said. "And check out their campfire first."

"No, let's split up," I said. "I'll go to Ravenwood. You check out our campfire. It'll be faster that way."

"Good plan!" Claire agreed.

We hurried off in opposite directions. I hiked around the lake towards the centre of Ravenwood's camp. When I got there, I noticed that all the Ravenwood kids were walking towards their main lodge.

I checked my watch, and my throat tightened. Not because it was almost dinnertime and I had to stop searching for the next clue, but because I was supposed to meet Rick and the Toadstools an hour ago to help teach them some songs!

In a panic, I raced back to Evergreen and ran to the Toadstool cabin. Empty.

I found them in the mess hall, already starting dinner. "I am so sorry!" I said to Rick. "We were doing the treasure hunt and I totally lost track of time."

"That's no excuse, Mary-Kate," Rick said. "I really could have used your help. If it happens again, I'm going to ask Nancy for another C.I.T."

What could I say? I knew he was right. I got myself a tray of chicken fingers and fries and sat at the end of the table next to Ben. "Hi, guys," I said, trying to show them that I was happy to be there.

Instead of saying hi, Ben sucked milk into his straw and blew it at me.

"Hey!" I ducked, but milk spurted all over my shirt anyway.

Ethan picked up the plastic bottle beside me and squeezed it. A splattering of mustard squirted into the air. Some of the spray landed on me.

"Marly-Cootie! Marly-Cootie!" Mojo chanted.

"Come on, you guys," I said. "That's not funny." *And quit calling me that!* I wanted to shout. But I was determined not to lose my temper. *I'll just ignore them*, I decided.

I reached for the salt to put some on my fries. The lid popped off with the first shake, and the whole container dumped onto my plate.

The boys burst out laughing.

So did Rick.

"I told you it'd be funny!" Big David whispered to Ethan. The boys had loosened the lid on purpose – to get me!

Stay calm. . . It's no big deal. . . be the grown-up. . . I repeated over and over inside my head.

But what can I say, Diary? The score was: boys 2, me 0.

Marly-Cootie was losing!

Making A Splash

Dear Diary,

Remember how I was supposed to meet Andrew tonight by the lake? Well, after dinner I went down there and waited for him.

And waited, and waited, and waited!

Where was he? We had a date. Did he forget?

A few kids from another cabin had come to skip stones into the water. Allison was with them.

"Have you seen Andrew?" I asked her.

"No," she answered with a sneeze. "Did you try the volleyball court?"

"Volleyball?" I repeated. Well, I guess it was worth a shot. "Thanks," I said and hiked up to the volleyball nets – just in case. No Andrew.

Then I went to his cabin, the main lodge, the campfire, and Evergreen Circle – this really cool circle of trees near the entrance to the camp. I couldn't find him anywhere.

Finally I trudged back down to the lake. Maybe I missed him. Maybe I left too soon or something. But he wasn't there.

I was just about to leave again, when I heard Andrew call my name. "Ashley!"

I turned to see him running towards me, waving. My heart skipped a beat. He *didn't* forget! "Hi!" I called back.

Then I saw who was behind him. Yup! Max and . . . *you-know-who.* The three of them were laughing hysterically.

"Sorry I'm late!" Andrew said. "Oh, my gosh, Ash. You should have seen what we just did!"

"It was awesome!" Max launched into the story. "We just sneaked into the kitchen, to grab some desserts. . ." He glanced Brooke.

"But then I got this brilliant idea!" Brooke said. "We saw this birthday cake sitting there, for Luke Pittman."

"Who?" I asked, feeling left out.

"He's one of the counsellors," Max explained, glancing at Brooke again.

"And his birthday is today," Andrew said. "I overheard some of the other counsellors talking about having a party for him after lights-out."

"So anyway, it had these candy letters on it, and I *dared* Max to switch them around. To change the writing on the cake," Brooke said.

"To what?" I asked.

"Happy Birthday, *Puke.*" Max burst out laughing again.

Typical gross-out joke, I thought. But it was kind of funny.

42

"Too bad you weren't there, Ash," Andrew said, chuckling.

"Yeah, *too bad*," Brooke said, but it didn't sound like she meant it.

"How come you didn't tell me about it?" I glanced at Andrew. "I was waiting for you."

I caught Brooke rolling her eyes.

"I mean, I could have come with you guys," I went on. "It sounds like it was fun."

"See?" Andrew turned to Brooke. "I *told* you she'd want to join us! Sorry, Ashley."

Huh? I stared at them.

"Brooke didn't think you'd want to be part of it," Max explained. "We didn't think it would take so long."

It figures, I thought. "Well, I definitely want to be there next time you guys pull a prank," I said.

Brooke gave me a sneaky-looking smile. "Are you *sure?*" she asked me.

Why not? I thought. *I'm not a chicken.* I stared right into Brooke's twinkling eyes. "Bring it on," I told her.

"Okay," she said. "But don't say I didn't warn you!"

Chapter 5

Thursday

Dear Diary,

Today was the big day. I finally got to pull a prank with Andrew, Max and Brooke. And you won't believe my luck!

It was the middle of the afternoon. Emily and I had just come back from the all-camp relay swim. Neither of us is a champion swimmer, so we were timing the races. I'm great with a stopwatch!

As we passed the trail that leads to the boys' cabins, I saw Andrew sneaking through the woods.

"Hey," I called to him. "What's up?"

Andrew looked around to be sure no one was watching. Then he motioned to me. "Come on. We've got a plan."

I glanced at Emily. "Do you mind?" I asked. I didn't want to leave her, but I did want to find out what the plan was.

"Oh, that's okay," Emily said. "You go on. I've got arts and crafts in fifteen anyway."

"Thanks, Em," I said and ran to join Andrew. I thought he was by himself. But then Brooke and Max emerged from behind a large tree.

"Ashley!" she said in her happy voice. "We were looking for you."

Yeah, I thought. *I'll bet.*

Brooke pulled a small jar of Tabasco sauce from her pocket. "You wanted to be in on this, right?" she said. "Here's your chance to make history."

She sounded a bit dramatic to me, but whatever. At least I wasn't being left out this time. "So what do I have to do?" I asked.

"We're putting Tabasco sauce in a counsellor's toothpaste," Max said with dancing eyes.

Hmmm. That didn't seem as funny and harmless as changing letters on a cake. Tabasco sauce is really spicy.

"You don't have to do it if you don't want to," Andrew said quickly. "It was Brooke's idea. She can do it."

"Yeah, Ash," Brooke cut in. "I'll do it."

"No, no, I want to do it!" I insisted. There was no way I was going to give Brooke an excuse to leave me out again!

Brooke handed me a long toothpick and the tiny jar of sauce. Then she led the way to a cabin at the top of the hill. "Go inside, put the Tabasco in the guy's toothpaste, and stir it with the toothpick."

"Okay," I said. But I felt a little weird about this. What if we got caught? I tried to put the thought out of my mind as I glanced around nervously. The coast was clear, so I slipped into the cabin quietly.

I found the counsellor's shelf, uncapped his toothpaste, and tried to put a few drops of the hot sauce inside the tube. Not an easy thing to do. The opening was very small.

"Whoa!" I whispered as the stuff dripped down the side of the tube and onto my fingers.

"Don't touch your eyes or it'll burn!" Andrew called from outside.

We shouldn't be doing this, I thought. *This prank is too mean.* I glanced at Brooke and Max outside the screened window.

"Come on! Hurry up!" Max called. "Someone's coming!"

What a mess! I screwed the cap on quickly and ran outside.

Whoops! I ran smack into Jeff Peters – the counsellor for that cabin. I barely knew him, but none of the kids in his cabin liked him.

"What's up, Ashley?" he asked.

But I didn't have to answer. He could see the little Tabasco jar in my hand. And two seconds later, he saw his tube of toothpaste covered with red sauce.

"Okay, it's kitchen duty for you," Jeff said. He took my arm and steered me towards the mess hall.

"You can peel a few hundred potatoes. Maybe that will get you to think about showing some respect for the people who make camp happen."

Max, Brooke and Andrew had already sneaked down the hill. I spotted them hiding behind a big bush.

Andrew and Max seemed truly upset that I'd got caught. But Brooke, well she just looked kind of bored.

I'll bet she planned this, I thought. *I'll bet Brooke wanted me to get in trouble – so I'd have to hang with two big bags of potatoes instead of my friends!*

So that's what I've been doing for hours, Diary. Sitting in this dumb kitchen, peeling potatoes!

Oh, and guess what else? Brooke, Max and Andrew dropped in to visit me in the kitchen after Jeff had left. They both offered to help, but Brooke dragged them away.

"Oh, no, we can't. We have to help set up the campfire. I think it's our turn to do it tonight," she said. "But don't worry," Brooke called. "I'll keep Andrew and Max company while you're here. So they won't be lonely."

Grrr!

The only good part was what Andrew did before he left. He had a small Camp Evergreen sticker on his shirt. He took it off and gently stuck it on my cheek.

I smiled when he touched my face. It was sort of like he was planting a kiss there!

Well, I'd better get back to work, Diary. I've still got another bag of spuds to go!

Diary, I just got back to my cabin and guess what? Something else is missing – a wildflower that Andrew picked for me one day when we were walking through the woods. It was on the shelf right next to my bed.

I was so excited when I got it. Everyone knows how much it meant to me. And now it's gone!

My heart is pounding because there's only one person who is mean enough to take it. One person who'd be happy if I'd never got the flower in the first place.

Brooke.

And you know what, Diary? I don't care if she's Andrew's best friend.

This is the last straw.

Making A Splash

Dear Diary,

I love the treasure hunt! And my friends and I rock! We solved the second clue this morning!

Mindy, Allison, Claire and I decided to spend the whole morning on it. And Brooke came along, too. Diary, Brooke is so much fun! I can't figure out why Ashley doesn't like her.

Mindy had to check her astrology charts before we began searching, of course. She said, "The stars tell me to stay close to home today. So let's look in Camp Evergreen."

Whatever makes her happy, I thought. I was just glad the stars didn't tell her to search in a garbage dump! Anyway, we read the clue again:

> IF YOU DON'T FIND THE NEXT CLUE,
> YOUR TEAM WILL BE TOAST.
> WANT S'MORE HELP?
> TRY THE CAMPFIRE ROAST!

"It's got to be near the campfire," Allison insisted. So we went there first to search. But we couldn't find anything.

"That clue about s'mores must mean something," Claire said. "Let's look for graham crackers or chocolate or marshmallows?"

"Sounds like a plan to me!" I said. "I'm always in the mood for s'mores." So we raced over to the mess hall. Patrick and his friend, Jason, were already there, going through the kitchen.

"You guys thinking the same thing we are?" Mindy asked.

Jason nodded and shot her a grin. "I guess so," he said.

I reached up to a shelf and pulled down a bag of marshmallows. It was sealed, but Patrick found one that was open. And the third clue was inside!

"Hey, Mary-Kate, look," Patrick said when he pulled the cardboard key out of the bag. "There's only one in here."

"Uh-oh." Brooke said. "That means Ravenwood is ahead of us. They must have got here first!"

Max walked in while we were talking. "What's up?" he asked Brooke.

"Ravenwood already has the third clue!" she said.

"We've got to catch up," Claire said. "Quick, Patrick. Read the new clue."

Patrick read it out loud. "'It's a sticky situation, to find the next clue. But stick with the birds, and you'll know what to do.'"

"Birds?" I said. "It must be on one of those raven-shaped signs that are plastered all over the place at Ravenwood."

"Let's go," Brooke said. "I know a shortcut."

I checked my watch. I was due to help Rick with the Toadstool boys in ten minutes. "I can't," I told everyone.

"You have to come," Allison said. "You were the one who figured it out."

"I know, but I'll help with the next clue," I promised.

"You'd better," Patrick said, shooting me a flirty smile.

My friends ran off and I headed out towards the big soccer field to meet Rick's little boys. Just as I reached it, I heard someone call my name. I turned and saw Jessie running toward me. She had been playing a game with her bunk mates at the edge of the field. Her new Big Sister – a girl named Rachel – was there, too.

"Hey!" I said, happy to see Jessie again.

"H-h-hi, Mary-Kate," Jessie said trying to catch her breath.

"Are you having fun with your new Big Sister?" I asked Jessie.

"Yup," Jessie said. "She's nice. She made this friendship bracelet for me. But she's not as much fun as you." She threw her arms around my legs and hugged me.

I hugged her back.

"Can you stay and play with us?" Jessie asked.

"Sorry," I said, shaking my head. "I have to go take care of those boys." I pointed to Rick's group, on the far side of the field. "But you know what?"

"What?" she asked.

I bent down and whispered, "If I had my choice, I'd much rather hang out with you!"

Rachel came over right then, so I said goodbye to Jessie and hurried to meet Rick and the Toadstools. When I got there, Rick was talking to Nancy. He had a clipboard in his hands.

Uh-oh, I thought nervously. I was already worried about messing up – especially with Nancy watching.

"Hi, Mary-Kate," Rick said quickly. "Can you keep an eye on them while I talk to Nancy? I'm making plans for the picnic lunch tomorrow."

"Okay." I nodded and took a deep breath. *Here goes*, I thought as I walked up to Ethan, Ben, Mojo and the three Davids.

"Ewww, here comes Marly-Cootie," one of them said.

They were running around wildly. So I thought I'd better get them playing some kind of game.

"Okay, guys. What do you want to do?" I asked.

"Football!" Ethan shouted, and the other guys joined in, shouting and jumping.

"You got it," I said. I ran over to a pile of balls and picked out a junior-size football. Finally something I'm good at. Sports are totally my thing. I glanced over at Nancy and Rick. Nancy was watching me out of the corner of her eye. *Maybe it's a good thing that she's here to see this*, I thought. *Maybe I can score some C.I.T. points!*

"Now, remember," I said to the guys. "This is just *touch* football. No tackling. Ethan, Mojo and Ben – you're on my team. The rest of you are on the other team. Ready?"

We lined up and Mojo hiked the football to Ethan. I ran down the field with Ben. Ethan threw the ball right to me, and I caught it.

"Get her!" one of the Davids yelled. They all rushed at me.

Even Ethan, Mojo and Ben!

"Hey – no!" I said. "You guys are on *my* team! You're not supposed to—" Before I could say the words *tackle me*, the boys knocked me to the ground.

"Get off!" I yelled. But I was trapped. Six boys were piled on top of me. Someone's knees were squishing my face. I could barely breathe. "Help!" I yelled, squirming to get free.

Mojo and Ben were laughing.

"All right, that's enough!" I heard Rick's super-firm voice. "Get off right now!"

They instantly jumped up.

I pulled myself to my feet and glanced at Nancy. She had seen the whole thing. "Thanks," I started to say to Rick. "Sorry I let them get out of control."

"You know what? Don't worry about it," he said, sounding a little fed up with me. "John is almost well enough to come back. He'll be back on Sunday. I think I can handle these guys on my own from here on." He blew his whistle and led the boys away.

My stomach turned into a big fat knot. Diary, how am I supposed to show Nancy – by Sunday – that I deserve the C.I.T. position if Rick doesn't even *want* my help anymore?

Maybe I *should* just quit.

Chapter 6

Friday

Dear Diary,

Okay. This is *really* the last straw. I'm not playing around any more. Remember the little Camp Evergreen sticker that Andrew gave me? Well, I put it right on top of my drawers and now it's gone. And I know Brooke took it!

How do I know? Right after morning swim, Emily and I had been working on the treasure hunt together. We ran over to Ravenwood and raided the cabins. Emily thought maybe there were some Raven signs inside. She was amazing! She sneaked right into Big Bob's office, too! But we didn't find anything.

We decided to head back to the cabin to change our clothes because it was so hot and we were all sweaty. Brooke brushed past us when we were walking up the steps. "Hey, Ashley," Brooke said in her fake-sweet voice. "What happened to the cute little sticker Andrew gave you? I thought you were never going to take it off."

I didn't think anything of it at the time, but right before lunch I noticed the sticker was missing. And my first thought was *Brooke*.

I wanted to talk to Emily about it, but she had gone to the director's cabin to call her parents before dinner.

And you know what, Diary? I'm tired of this. I'm tired of everyone thinking Brooke is fun and cool and nice when she's none of those things.

I ran out of the bunk and over to the mess hall. Allison, Claire, Mary-Kate and Mindy were sitting at a table together.

"What's the matter?" Mary-Kate said when she saw me. "What's wrong?"

"Brooke's been stealing my stuff," I said.

Mindy stopped with a ham sandwich halfway to her mouth. "Are you kidding me?"

I shook my head. "She's been taking things off my corkboard and out of my drawers."

"Wow," Allison said. "Did you see her do it?"

"No, but I *know* it was her," I said.

"How?" Mindy asked.

"I just know," I replied. What could I say? I couldn't actually prove it.

"Are you serious, Ashley?" Claire sounded kind of angry. "How would you like it if Brooke told everyone *you* stole stuff and she had no proof?"

"Yeah," Allison muttered.

This was unreal! My friends were staring at me as if *I* were in the wrong! "But she's got you all fooled," I started to say. "She's not as nice as—" I stopped.

Brooke walked into the mess hall and sat down

with us. "Hi!" she said, all cheery. "Hey, Allison. Do you realise I've been here five days? And you still haven't told me a secret you've never told anyone else. Remember?"

"I'm still thinking about it," Allison answered.

Mary-Kate got up and pulled me aside. "Ash, what's with you?" she asked.

"Nothing! I'm just mad at Brooke!" I whispered.

"Come on. Do you really think Brooke would steal your stuff?" Mary-Kate asked.

"Well, no one else would take my picture of Andrew!" I said. "Or the sticker he gave me."

"How do you know?" Mary-Kate asked. "Or maybe you just misplaced those things," she added. "I can help you look around later, if you want."

My shoulders slumped. I knew she was right. I shouldn't have blamed Brooke without proof.

"Listen. I've got to go," Mary-Kate said. "Rick came by while I was playing volleyball. He changed his mind. He really *didn't* want to handle the little

monsters alone. So he asked me to help out at the huge picnic they're having for the younger kids by the lake today."

"Sure. See you later," I said. I slinked back to the table and joined the rest of the bunk.

But it wasn't fun. Everyone was mad at me and I had to pretend that Brooke was as innocent as apple pie. How fair is *that?*

Dear Diary,

I have to figure out a way to get Ashley to come around about Brooke. She's thinks that Brooke is out to get her, and I don't know why.

In the meantime, let me tell you what happened at the picnic today. For some reason, when I got there the Toadstool boys were being nice to me.

"Hi, Mary-Kate," Ben said.

Huh? I thought. How come he didn't call me Marly-Cootie?

"You want to sit with us?" Mojo scooted over on his bench to make room.

I sat down, but I was still wondering what was up. *Maybe they feel bad for tackling me yesterday,* I thought.

Then Ethan got up and walked around the table. He had a paper plate with a sandwich on it. "Here," he said. "We saved lunch for you."

"Thanks!" My stomach was growling since I didn't eat lunch with my bunk mates. I picked up the sandwich and started to take a bite. That's when I noticed the worm wiggling around near the edge of the bread!

"Ewww!" I dropped the sandwich fast.

"Ha-ha-haaaaa!" Ethan laughed.

And Ben almost spit out his milk, he was giggling so hard.

"Okay, that's it!" I jumped up from the table. I mean, how much can a girl take? "I'm going to the rest room. I'll be right back," I told Rick – mostly so I could take a walk and cool down. When I reached the path, I spotted Jessie coming toward me.

"Mary-Kate!" she said, happy to see me.

"Hey." I guess I sounded pretty glum.

"You look sad," she said. "You want a piece of candy? Rachel gave me these."

Jessie pulled a Gummi Worm from a bag and handed it to me. But it wasn't a regular red-yellow-blue Gummi Worm. It was one of those special ones – the kind that are brown and slimy-looking. The kind that looked real!

The moment I saw it, I knew exactly what to do. "Thanks, Jessie! This is just what I need!"

I hid the candy worm in my hand and ran back to the Toadstools' table. Luckily, the boys were busy throwing paper napkins at each other. They didn't pay any attention to me.

I grabbed a new peanut butter sandwich and stuck the fake worm in between the bread so that it peeked out from the edge of the sandwich.

"Hey, guys," I said. "I'm hungry enough to eat a horse! But since there aren't any horses around here, I guess I'll have to settle for this worm." I made sure they saw the worm. Then I bit into the sandwich – eating the whole thing in three big bites!

"Ewwww!" the smallest David said.

But the rest of the boys thought I was awesome! They cheered.

That was so easy, I thought, laughing. *Why didn't I think of it before?*

From now on, I knew exactly what I had to do. Forget laying down the rules. Just make sure these guys had fun. That's what camp was all about! And as long as I kept them from being too wild, everyone would be happy. Rick, Nancy *and* the boys.

After I ate that worm, the boys seemed as if they would follow me anywhere – and do whatever I told them.

I didn't get a chance to try it out, though, because a minute later Ashley came running up. "Mary-Kate! You've got to come quick!" she cried. "We've got a huge problem!"

I got a sick feeling as I ran to my sister. *What's wrong?* I wondered. *What could it possibly be?*

Chapter 7

Friday

Dear Diary,

I saw it with my own eyes! Two creeps from Ravenwood – Pete and Shawna – sneaked over to Camp Evergreen and stole back the portrait of the McArdle sisters!

"How did it happen?" Mary-Kate asked me after I told her the awful story. "Wasn't anyone guarding it?"

"Allison and some guy they call the Hulk from Andrew's cabin were there. They were *supposed* to be guarding it," I told her. "But Allison had a sneezing fit. She went to the bathroom for more tissues. And I guess Pete held down the Hulk while Shawna took the painting."

"But couldn't you stop them?" Mary-Kate asked.

That's what everyone's been asking me ever since! Like I'm supposed to stop a guy who's bigger and stronger than the Hulk!

"I tried, but they were already running away when I saw them. They ran around the lake during the kids' picnic. I yelled for them to stop. And called people to help me chase them, but no one heard me."

Mary-Kate nodded. She knows how loud it can get at the waterfront – especially when the little kids are playing.

"Well, we have to get it back!" she said.

"Tell me about it," I said. That's when we decided to call a meeting tonight to make a plan.

Oops! Gotta run, Diary. I'm supposed to meet Andrew in a few minutes – without Brooke. Finally! More later.

Dear Diary,

Here's the deal. Camp Evergreen is *not* doing well in the treasure hunt. We still haven't figured out that bird clue. If we lose the hunt, then we lose the whole inter-camp competition.

So getting back the portrait is major. And I'm not leaving Camp Evergreen until we find it. Even if I have to stay through the winter!

Claire and I decided to sneak over to Ravenwood after lunch today – just to find out where the painting was hanging. Luckily, my little Toadstools were having a rest period, so Rick didn't need me.

We hiked through the woods to the other camp. On the way, we passed a bunch of Evergreen kids, coming back, including Patrick. "You going to look for the portrait?" he asked.

I nodded.

"Good luck," he said, sounding frustrated. "We couldn't find it anywhere!"

"Where did you look?" I asked.

"Everywhere, practically. Except in the trunk of Big Bob's car," Patrick joked.

"It's not in their camp, man," one of the other kids said. "I'm telling you – they must be cheating or something."

Claire and I wanted to see for ourselves. We tramped through the thick part of the woods and came out on Ravenwood territory.

"Let's check out the lodge anyway," she said. "I just can't believe they didn't put it back where it always hangs."

So we headed into the Ravenwood main lodge and stared at all the walls. Lots of banners and signs were plastered all over the place. But the big space over the stone fireplace was empty. No painting.

"You'll never find it," someone behind us said in that *nah-nah-nah* tone of voice.

I whirled around. There was Shawna, Pete's friend. She had her arms crossed and she was leaning against the doorway.

"That's what *you* think," I said. "It's just a matter of time."

"Right. Like all the time you need to solve the treasure hunt clues?" she said. "I mean, seriously! We figured out the third clue hours ago!"

Claire and I glanced at each other.

Shawna pretended to yawn. "Well, I guess I'll go

take a nap before I solve the fourth clue," she said as she strolled out of the lodge.

"Come on," Claire said. "Let's look around."

I'm telling you, Diary, we searched everywhere. But that painting was not to be found! Finally we hurried back to Evergreen and found a bunch of our friends huddled by Evergreen Circle.

"The portrait is nowhere," Claire said. "And Ravenwood is on their fourth clue of the treasure hunt!"

"So are we!" Mindy cried happily. "We just found it!" She held up a black cardboard key.

"Where?" I was glad and disappointed at the same time. I had wanted to be part of the team that found it.

"It was hidden in one of those birdhouses in the arts-and-crafts cabin," Emily said. "You know – the ones made out of Popsicle sticks."

"Ohhh," I said. I thought back to the clue. *Sticky situation. . . stick with the birds. . .* "Cool."

"Emily found it," Allison said, smiling.

"So what does the next clue say?" Claire asked.

Emily read from the key: "'The next clue is easy, it's not really two words. It's been here forever, this clue is for the birds.'"

64

"Birds again?" I said.

Claire stamped her foot. "No fair! We just got done searching every stupid bird flag and bird sign at Ravenwood!"

"Maybe it's in another one of those birdhouses," Allison said. "We didn't look in all of them."

I doubted it. But we raced back to the arts-and-crafts cabin anyway, to look. Nope.

So now what, Diary? We don't have the portrait. Ravenwood is ahead of us in the treasure hunt. And the clues are getting harder! Help!

Dear Diary,

It's Friday night and I'm not going to the old black-and-white movie they're showing in the lodge after dinner. I'm not going to the campfire tonight, either. You see, I'm not allowed to do those things. Instead, I have to sit here all by myself – as punishment!

Let me tell you what happened. This afternoon Andrew and I planned to go to the lake – alone – and figure out where the Ravenwood kids could have hidden the portrait. But right before I was supposed to leave to meet him, I ran into Brooke.

"Can I come?" Brooke asked me. She and Mindy and Allison had just walked into the cabin.

"Um, I think Andrew and I want to go by ourselves," I said. "A big group will attract too much attention." Which was true, if you thought about it.

"Okay," Brooke agreed, sounding really nice and friendly. "But I just came up with an awesome idea for another prank."

"Oh, you should hear her ideas!" Mindy said, excited. "This afternoon she wanted to paint hearts on the targets at the archery course!"

That *did* sound kind of fun. And cute. I had to admit it. Everyone shooting arrows would be like cupids.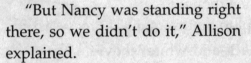

"But Nancy was standing right there, so we didn't do it," Allison explained.

"So what's your new prank?" I asked.

Brooke's eyes danced. "It's a secret," she said. "I won't tell – unless you guys are going to help."

Claire shook her head. "Sorry. I'm working on the treasure hunt this afternoon."

Mindy nodded. "Me, too."

"Sorry," I said to Brooke. "I'm out." I started for the door, but Brooke called me back.

"Oh, Ashley, there was a note for you taped to the screen." She gave it to me.

It was from Andrew. I read the note twice. It said:

Making A Splash

Hey, Ash,
My dad wants me to put in an extra tennis
practice today. Can we hang out later? At
campfire? I'll toast a marshmallow just for
you! Sorry!

Love, Andrew

Bummer! I *so* wanted to hang out with him. But at least he signed the note *Love!*

Brooke was reading over my shoulder. "Sounds like you're free this afternoon after all," she said with a smile.

Yeah, I guess so, I thought.

"You still want to do this prank?" Brooke asked.

"Maybe . . ." I hesitated. "What is it?"

"Come on. I'll show you," she said, grabbing her backpack and heading out the door.

I followed her, not knowing where we were going. She led me to the laundry shack. It was a small log building filled with huge washers and dryers. That's where all the sheets and towels for the camp were washed.

"So, what's the prank?" I asked when we got there. The door was open, but no one was inside.

"This." Brooke reached into her backpack and pulled out a brand-new red T-shirt. "We'll toss it in with the white sheets. They'll all turn pink!"

That's not fun, I thought. *Maybe* I'd *like pink sheets, but I'll bet not all the guys' cabins would.* "No thanks," I said. "I'm not up for that one."

Brooke rolled her eyes and sighed. "I knew you weren't like me and Andrew and Max. You're so boring." Then, with a huff, she stomped into the laundry shack and tossed the T-shirt into a load of whites. She slipped out just a second before Tom, the laundry guy, came around the corner.

"What's going on?" he asked, eyeing us.

"Nothing," Brooke said, starting to walk away.

I followed her. I didn't want to get in trouble for something I didn't do!

But I guess Tom knew she was lying, because he ran inside and quickly checked out the washers. Then he came running after us. "Hold on, you two," he said, grabbing us both by the arms. "Who put that red T-shirt in with the white sheets?"

"*She* did it!" Brooke said, pointing at me.

Chapter 8

Saturday

Dear Diary,

I don't know how Brooke convinced Tom that I was the one who pulled the prank yesterday, but she did. And I had to pay for it last night. It was then that I decided to give Andrew the scoop on his not-as-nice-as-he-thinks-she-is friend, Brooke.

I found him after morning swim and took him aside. "Andrew, we have to talk," I said.

"Hey." He gave me a strange stare. "What's going on? Are you mad at me or something?"

"Where did you get *that* idea?" I asked.

"Well, you didn't come to campfire last night," he said.

I rolled my eyes. "I wanted to be there, but I couldn't – because of Brooke!" I launched into the whole story about the prank and how she pinned it on me. Then I gave him the scoop on how Brooke always cut me out of conversations. And how she seemed as if she didn't want me to be friends with Max and him. I wanted to mention that she'd been stealing my stuff, too. But I couldn't prove that yet! So I didn't say any more.

"She's got a serious problem with me, but I don't know what it is," I said. "And I don't care."

Andrew seemed surprised. But he couldn't deny that it was pretty ratty of Brooke to blame *me* for the pink-sheet stuff. "To tell you the truth, she has been saying a few things about you," he admitted.

Unbelievable! "Like what?" I asked.

"Just stuff about how we'd have more fun without you," Andrew said. "I could never figure out why. Maybe she's jealous or something."

"Jealous?" I said. "Why? She's smart and pretty and she has a ton of friends. Why would she be jealous of me?"

Andrew smiled. "Lots of reasons. But if Brooke wants to play that way, she's going to be sorry."

"What do you mean?" I asked him.

His smile turned into a sneaky grin. "If she wants other people to take the heat for her pranks, fine. Now she's going to get a taste of her own medicine."

I tried to imagine what Andrew was up to. But none of it would be as good as catching Brooke stealing my things.

"You know what?" I said. "I'll handle this. I've got a plan of my own."

After a game of volleyball, Mary-Kate and I went back to the cabin to talk about what I wanted to do. After she had found out about Brooke's prank, Mary-Kate was totally onboard with some payback.

"So I want to set a trap for her," I said.

"What kind of trap?" Mary-Kate whispered. The two of us were standing outside our cabin, under some pine trees. Everyone else was getting dressed.

"I'm going to put Andrew's note out where Brooke can see it," I said. "She's been stealing my other stuff, so maybe she'll take the bait. And maybe we'll can catch her at it."

"Okay," Mary-Kate agreed. "Brooke's in the shower, so let's do it now."

We slipped into the cabin. Allison and Claire were there, lounging on their bunks.

"Where should I put it?" I asked Mary-Kate.

"Just leave it on your bed," Mary-Kate said. "Where she'll notice it right away."

"Notice what? Who?" Claire asked.

"Brooke," I said. "It's about time I proved she's been stealing my stuff. I'm going to catch her in the act."

Claire and Allison stopped what they were doing and came over. "What's going on?" Allison asked.

I told them everything. About the way Brooke blamed me for the pink sheets. And how she's been saying bad stuff about me. And how she's been taking all the special things Andrew gave me.

"Wow," Claire said. "She seemed so nice!"

"Believe me," I said. "She's not."

"But do you have proof this time?" Allison asked. "Because you can't just go accusing people. . . ."

"I have proof that she blamed me for something she did! And Andrew is the one who said she's been talking about me," I argued. "And now I'm going to get proof that she's a thief." I put Andrew's note on my pillow.

"Do you really think Brooke will take that?" Claire asked.

"We'll find out," I said. "But everyone can see it's here, right? So when she steals it, you'll all be witnesses."

Just then the screen door hinge squeaked. I looked over and saw Brooke standing in the doorway, in her robe. How long had she been there?

"You all think I'm a thief?" She looked as if she might cry.

I gulped. She'd been standing there long enough. I didn't know what to say. Because the answer was yes! I did think that!

"Well, *did* you take Ashley's stuff?" Claire asked.

Tears began to stream down Brooke's face. She threw her towel and soap on the floor of the cabin. Then she turned and ran off down the path.

"Uh-oh," Mary-Kate turned to me. "Are you *sure* she did it?"

Before I could answer, Emily entered the cabin.

She had been standing outside, behind Brooke. She had witnessed the whole thing. "Ashley, can I talk to you in private?" she asked.

"Not now," I said. I was kind of worried about Brooke, wondering if maybe I had been wrong.

"No, I need to talk to you *now*," Emily said. "Please!" She crossed the room to her bunk and grabbed something from her shelf. It was wrapped in a pink pillowcase. Then she motioned for me to follow her. She ducked into a little private alcove where our counsellor Jill's bed is.

"I made this for you." Emily handed me the pillowcase. "It's a thank-you gift, because you've been such a good friend to me at camp."

I opened the pillowcase—and guess what was inside, Diary? A beautiful friendship scrapbook! Similar to the one Emily had brought from home.

Only this had all kinds of things about me in it. There were poems and drawings and photos . . . and all of the things from Andrew that I thought Brooke had stolen!

The photograph, the wildflower, and the sticker. They were all there.

"Oh, no!" I gasped.

"I took those things for your scrapbook," Emily

said. "I didn't think you'd notice them missing so fast. And I *never* thought you'd blame Brooke."

I gave Emily a hug. "Thank you, Emily," I said. "This is really, really great!" Normally I would have been totally thrilled, but I wasn't. Because even though Brooke isn't what you'd call the nicest girl in the world, I felt awful about accusing her of stealing in front of everybody.

I knew I had to apologise to her. I just had to figure out a way to do it.

Dear Diary,

Today I was determined to solve that fourth clue of the treasure hunt. Ashley couldn't help me because she went looking for Brooke. So Mindy, Jason, Patrick and I put our heads together.

"I give up," Mindy said after we had spent the whole afternoon searching for bird things.

"Don't quit yet," Jason said to her. "We just have to think harder." He kept saying the clue, over and over. "'The next clue is easy – it's not really two words. It's been here forever – this clue is for the birds.'"

"It's not easy to me," Mindy said.

"I know!" I agreed. "We've thought of every-thing! We searched the bushes that have berries the birds like to eat. We looked at every bird picture at Ravenwood again. We even looked in the big bags of birdseed. Nothing."

"Hey – maybe it's easier than that! What about the Ravenwood sign at the front of the camp?" Patrick said.

"But there's no picture of a bird on it," Mindy argued.

"So what?" Jason said. "The clue says 'It's not really two words.' And *Ravenwood* isn't two words – right?"

They ran over to Camp Ravenwood, searched the big sign, and guess what? That's where the next clue was!

The only problem is that the Ravenwood kids solved that clue right away. They've had the fifth clue for a whole day!

Jason read the fifth clue to us: "'Oh, say can you see that your friends will all rave. For this star-spangled summer – long may it wave. Solve this riddle and you'll find the treasure!'"

I was pumped. At least we were back in the race for the treasure!

"It's something about a flag," Mindy said.

"Definitely," I agreed.

"So, let's go," Patrick said. "There are a bunch of flags at both camps."

We started to take off on the hunt. But then I checked my watch. "It's almost dinnertime," I said. "We have to stop the hunt." And besides, I had to go help Rick with the Toadstool boys. So we all made plans to get up really early tomorrow. We're going to start searching the flags before breakfast!

I hurried to the mess hall to find the Toadstool boys. And today not a single one of them spat milk, threw napkins or spilled ketchup on me.

"Nice going," Rick said when dinner was almost over. "Too bad John is coming back tomorrow. You turned out to be pretty good at this C.I.T. thing."

"Thanks!" I said, feeling proud.

After dinner I decided to do one last good deed – just to prove to myself that I was handling the boys really well. "Hey, guys," I said. "Let's clean up the mess hall, okay?"

"Naahhh," Mojo said.

"No way," Ben added.

I quickly arranged a bunch of rubbish bins in the middle of the floor. "Two points for every piece of garbage that hits the basket!" I said. I crumpled up a paper plate that some-one had left on the floor, and tossed it.

Swish! It went right in.

"Two points for me!" I cheered, grabbing some more rubbish.

Right away the kids started tossing rubbish into the bins.

"Two points!" Ben shouted.

"This is a three-pointer!" Ethan cried.

Mojo scrambled around the empty dining hall, looking for stuff to throw into the cans.

Within minutes the place was spotless.

"Thanks, guys," I said as I led them towards the door. Then I noticed Nancy standing near the entrance. She'd been watching me the whole time.

"Nice job, Mary-Kate," she said. "That was impressive."

"Thanks!" I said, beaming.

Nancy nodded and smiled. "You're going to make an excellent C.I.T. next year. You've got the job."

"Yes!" I cheered, pushing a fist into the air.

Isn't that great, Diary? I'll be coming back to Evergreen! Now all we have to do is find the treasure – and the portrait – and this will be a perfect summer!

Chapter 9

Sunday

Dear Diary,

I tried to talk to Brooke alone last night, but she wouldn't even look at me during dinner. Or at campfire.

And she didn't come back to the cabin till lights out. No way was I going to have a talk with her in front of everyone else. That would never work.

So, I got up early this morning. I waited for Mary-Kate, Mindy and the others to leave. When Brooke was alone, I didn't waste any time. "Brooke," I said, "can we talk?"

She didn't answer. She started braiding her hair.

"I'm sorry about yesterday," I went on. "I was so wrong to accuse you of stealing. Emily did it. She made me a scrapbook."

"I heard," Brooke said. She kept braiding.

"I was all wrong about that," I admitted. "But you *did* try to get Andrew and Max to stop hanging out with me. And you *did* blame me for that pink-sheet prank. That was wrong, too."

Brooke swung around and looked me right in the eye. "You're right," she said. "I didn't want you hanging with my friends anymore. You were totally ruining everything."

"Me?" I was shocked. "How?"

Making A Splash

"First it was like you were taking my place. And then you wanted Andrew all to yourself!" she replied. "You never wanted me and Max around. And we were friends with him first!"

"No, I just . . ." I started to say. But then I thought about it. Okay, maybe it was true – a little. "But I wasn't trying to break up your friendship," I explained. "I just wanted to have some time alone with my boyfriend. What's wrong with that?"

"Nothing, I guess." Brooke nodded slowly.

"How come you never let us do that?" I asked.

"Maybe I was afraid that if Andrew had a girlfriend, he wouldn't want to hang out with me anymore."

I nodded. It kind of made sense now. "Well, maybe we can try being friends," I told her. "I mean, that's what I wanted in the first place."

"Yeah. I'm tired of being rude," she said. "It isn't my style, Ashley. Really."

"Me either," I said. "So let's call a truce." And I'm so glad we did. Because, Diary, I have an idea for the greatest prank of all time. If I pull this off, Brooke will have no doubt about whether I'm her friend.

Dear Diary,

Hold on to your pages, because I am about to tell you something truly amazing.

79

We found the McArdle portrait!!!

We weren't even looking for it. We were working on that clue about flags for the treasure hunt.

Claire was taking charge, as usual. "Mary-Kate, you search the flagpole in Evergreen Circle. Mindy, check out the flags in the main lodge. Emily, go see if there's a flag in Nancy's office. Then we'll meet up and check out the flags hanging from each cabin."

"What are you and Allison going to do?" I asked.

"We're going to check out every single American flag and pole we can find at Ravenwood," Claire said.

"We'll meet at the lodge in an hour," Mindy said.

So that's what we did. I searched every inch of that main flagpole in Evergreen Circle – but all I found was a coin in the sand.

I was walking back towards the cabins, when I ran into Rick and John. They were playing a game of dodge ball with the boys from Toadstool.

"Hi, Mary-Kate!" Ben called out. He was sitting on the sidelines because he was already out of the game.

"Hi, Ben," I said.

"Hey, Mary-Kate!" Mojo ran over, and some of the other guys followed him.

"Where were you?" Ethan asked. "We want you on our team!"

Awww! I thought. That's so nice! They want me to hang around with them even though John is back!

"I've been working on a treasure hunt," I told him. "We're trying to beat Ravenwood."

I told them about the clues, then I read them the last one.

"I don't get it," Mojo said.

"Well, those are the first words to the *'Star-spangled Banner,'*" I said.

"So it's a flag!" Ben yelled.

I nodded. "That's what we think. But we looked at every single flag in both camps and we can't find the treasure."

"Maybe it's not a flag," Ethan said. "Maybe it's one of those big camp banners hanging in the mess hall."

"Yeah!" I said, jumping up. "Maybe you're right."

I dashed off to meet Claire and everyone else. I told them what Ethan had said.

"It's worth a try," Claire agreed.

Mindy and Emily went to search the banners in Evergreen's lodge. Claire and I hurried over to Ravenwood.

When we reached their lodge, we acted as if we were just hanging out there because we were tired. Luckily, no one was around. It wasn't lunchtime or dinner. Two young boys were reading comic books at the far end. But they left when they saw us. They acted as if they wanted to get away from us because we were creepy girls.

Cool, I thought. *Now we can search the place!*

We gazed at the banners hanging high overhead on the rafters.

"Hand me that broomstick." Claire pointed to one that was propped up near a fireplace.

I did, and she used it to poke behind the banners. But there were no clue keys hidden up there. At least we couldn't see any. We checked the banners hanging on the walls, too. Nothing.

There was only one last banner, high over the door to the Ravenwood dining hall. Claire had to stand on a chair and use the broomstick. She lifted the banner away from the wall and gasped. "Look!"

I craned my neck to see a painting of two stiff-looking ladies with greying hair. The portrait! "Can you get it?" I asked.

Claire tried knocking it down with the broom, but she stopped. She didn't want to damage it. "I'll bet it's been hanging up there all along! Ever since they stole it." She jumped down from the chair, and we hurried back to Evergreen to tell our friends we found the portrait.

Now all we had to do was get it back!

Chapter 10

Monday

Dear Diary,

The plan was simple. We hiked to Ravenwood superearly and got there right before the campers arrived at their lodge for breakfast.

We had divided into two teams. Ashley, Andrew, Max and Brooke were one team. My team was Patrick, Jason and me.

Ashley peeked in the window of their lodge. Two older girls were sitting at a table. "I think they're guarding the painting," she whispered.

"No problem," I said. I had borrowed some plastic puke from Mojo. I handed it to Brooke. "You know what to do, right?"

Brooke nodded, and Ashley's team strolled into the lodge. When the Ravenwood girls weren't looking, Brooke dropped the plastic vomit on the floor. Then she acted sick to her stomach.

"Ohhhhhhhhh!" Brooke gagged and pretended to hurl.

The Ravenwood girls rushed to her. "Are you okay?" one of them asked. They had their backs to the hidden painting.

"Noooooooo," Brooke moaned. "I feel awful." She hurled again.

"We got it!" Ashley cried. "Come on!" She and Andrew ran out of the lodge, holding what looked like a painting covered with a sheet. But it wasn't the McArdle portrait, Diary. It was a piece of board we borrowed from the arts-and-crafts cabin!

But Brooke was totally having fun with her sick act. "I think I might lose it again," she said, standing near the fake puke.

"Brooke! Let's go!" Max yelled. He dragged her away. "We've got the *painting!*"

Finally she bolted out of there and the four of them tore down the path to Evergreen.

"Stop them!" The Ravenwood girls ran outside after Ashley's team. "They're stealing the painting!"

About half the kids at Ravenwood were on their way to the lodge right then. As soon as they saw Ashley, Andrew, Max and Brooke, they started chasing them.

"Get them!" everyone shouted. "They've got the painting!"

Of course the painting was still on the wall in the lodge! The Ravenwood kids were chasing Ashley's team for nothing. Only they didn't know that!

That's when my team went to work, Diary. Patrick and Jason pulled a table over to the doorway. They stood on it. Then Jason climbed onto Patrick's shoulders. He took the portrait down from behind the banner.

"Hurry!" I whispered. Then our team dashed out of the back door and into the woods. We took the long way around to Evergreen.

When Ashley's team arrived at Evergreen, she told me what had happened. "They tackled us in the soccer field," she said, laughing. "You wouldn't believe how mad Pete and Shawna were when they found out that they'd been tricked!"

"What did they say?" I asked.

"Not much," Ashley answered. "But Andrew gave them the board and said, 'Why don't you hang this in the lodge? 'Cause you're never getting the painting back.' Then Pete said that the summer wasn't over and that we're going to lose the treasure hunt *and* the McArdle portrait."

So now we have *two* missions for the rest of the week, Diary. We have to make sure Ravenwood doesn't steal the portrait back. And we have to figure out clue number five of the treasure hunt before Ravenwood does!

Dear Diary,

I think Brooke and I are going to be friends now that we understand each other. We had a great time stealing the portrait back from Ravenwood. You should have seen Brooke pretending to puke. I swear, that girl should win an Academy Award for that performance.

I can't wait to show her how good an actress *I* am when I pull a trick on *her.* But more on that later.

After we got the portrait, Max sweet-talked the cooks into giving us a cooler full of lemonade and some cookies so a bunch of us could have a picnic down by the dock. We enjoyed the sun while the younger kids had swimming classes on the lake.

"Now, if only we could solve the fifth clue, we'd win everything," I said.

"Uh-oh. Look behind you," Mindy told me.

We all turned to see what Mindy was staring at. Jessie, Mary-Kate's used-to-be Little Sister, was walking towards us in her bathing suit. She had a big smile on her face. She threw her arms around Mary-Kate's neck when she reached us.

"Hi!" Jessie said.

"Hi, Jessie," Mary-Kate said. "What's up?"

"I just learned how to dive!" Jessie said.

"That's cool, Jessie!" Mary-Kate said. "I bet you're really good at it, too." She picked up a choco-late chip cookie. "Want one?"

"Yeah!" Jessie said. She took it and shoved the whole thing in her mouth at once. "What are you guys doing?" she mumbled as she tried to chew.

Mary-Kate told her all about the treasure hunt. "We're trying to solve the last clue," she said. "And when we do, we'll win everything! Isn't that cool?"

Jessie's eyes lit up. "I can help! My mom says I'm great at finding things. Once I found twenty-three cents in the couch at home and Dad let me keep it!"

"Well," Mary-Kate said. "It's really only for the older campers."

"Oh, come on," Andrew said, laughing a little. "Let's give her a chance. If we don't win the treasure hunt, maybe we'll find some change."

He pulled out the key and read the clue to Jessie. "'Oh, say, can you see, that your friends will all rave. For this star-spangled summer, long may it wave!'"

"Huh?" Jessie frowned.

"We think it's got to be an American flag," Claire explained to Jessie.

"But we've looked at all the flags in both camps," Brooke said.

"Did you look at his flag?" Jessie asked, pointing at Corey, the lifeguard, who was wearing a baseball cap – the same cap he  wore every single day. A cap with the Stars and Stripes on it!

"Oh, wow!" Mary-Kate cried. "Why didn't we think of that?"

We all jumped up and ran as fast as we could to the lifeguard chair.

I got there first. "Hey, Corey, can you come down for a minute?" I asked.

"Yup." Corey motioned for another lifeguard to watch the water, then hopped off his chair.

"Can I see your hat?" I asked.

Cory grinned and bent his head. I plucked it off. Inside his hat was a note.

"We did it!" I cried as I read it. "'Congratulations! You've found the treasure! It's buried in the sand under this lifeguard's chair!'"

"Yeah!" Jason cheered.

"Evergreen rocks!" Max screamed.

"Tree Frogs rock!" Emily cried.

"No, *Jessie* rocks!" Mary-Kate said.

Mary-Kate and I fell to our knees in the sand and started digging. Everyone else joined in, too. Jessie was digging the hardest and fastest! But her hands were little.

"I feel it!" Jason said as his hand hit something hard. A minute later, he pulled out a small metal box.

We all made a circle around him as he opened it.

"Here's a note," Jason said. "And a DVD or a movie."

"What movie?" Max asked.

"*Sorority Vampire!*" Jason said.

"All right!" everyone shouted.
That was a funny new horror
movie that we all wanted to see.

"Read the note!" Claire said,
excited.

The note said that we'd won the treasure hunt.
And as a prize, we all got to have a movie party in
the lodge.

"Awesome!" Brooke said. "We're going to have
so much fun!"

"Jessie – you're the best!" Mary-Kate cheered.
She lifted Jessie and swung her around.

I was so happy, I wanted to leap into Andrew's
arms. But I didn't. I just smiled at him. I still hadn't
told him about my secret plan for Brooke.

But now that we'd won the treasure hunt – and
the McArdle portrait was where it belonged – this
prank was the very next thing on my list!

Chapter 11

Tuesday

Dear Diary,

Tonight was the big night – Get-Brooke Night.

Andrew and I were at our spot by the lake when I told him about my plan to pull the best prank ever on Brooke. But not the whole plan. That was a surprise for him, too.

"So what did you tell her?" he asked me.

"I just said that I knew some guy liked her," I replied. "And that he wants to meet her down by the lake tonight at eight."

"And she fell for it?" Andrew asked.

"Yup," I nodded.

Andrew grinned. "And then no one will show up, right?" He laughed. "She'll look like a fool. She deserves it!"

I smiled. "Wait and see," I said.

"Huh?" He looked confused.

"Don't worry about it," I told him. "Let's go down there, where we can see her," I said, pointing to the dock. "I think you'll be surprised."

So that's what we did, Diary. Andrew and I found a good hiding spot by some pine trees near the boathouse.

The sky wasn't dark yet, but the sun was almost

down. A large half-moon shone overhead. Brooke was already there when we showed up. She was sitting on the dock, dangling her feet in the water.

We sat in a bed of pine needles, under the tree branches. I checked my watch. It was almost eight. *Is it going to work?* I wondered.

Then I spotted my secret weapon. Max. He was walking towards the dock with a smile on his face.

"What's up?" Andrew asked me. "Max is in on this, too?"

I laughed softly. "I told Max the same thing I told Brooke," I explained. "I said that some girl liked him and that she wanted to meet him here."

Andrew blinked. "How come?"

"Because it's true!" I whispered. "Haven't you noticed? Max is totally crazy about Brooke! And I think she likes him, too. If they get together, then the four of us can have so much fun!"

Andrew grinned at me. "You're nice," he said, leaning close to my face and touching his forehead to mine.

"Listen." I nodded towards Brooke and Max.

"Max, you've got to go," Brooke said, standing. "Ashley said there's a guy at camp who likes me. I'm meeting someone here."

"Wait a sec. Ashley said a girl wanted to meet *me* here," Max answered.

"She set this up?" Brooke said. She took a step closer to Max. "Um, was she telling the truth? Are you the guy who likes me?"

Max blushed. "Totally," he said with a shy smile. "But I didn't tell her. I don't know how she knows."

"Who cares? I like you, too," Brooke said. Then she looked as if she had just had a great idea. "Let's do something fun," she said. "Something wild and crazy."

"Really?" Max said, teasing her with a grin. "You really want me to do something crazy?" He stepped towards her.

Brooke stepped back on the dock. She looked over her shoulder at the water.

I held my breath. Was he going to push her in?

"Go ahead," she said. "I dare you."

Max stepped forward again. But he didn't push her. He grabbed her arms and kissed her!

"Wow," Andrew said. "That was pretty crazy."

"Too crazy?" I asked.

"Nope," Andrew said. Then he did the same thing! He leaned over and kissed me.

I almost melted!

After that, we jumped up and joined Max and Brooke. Then we all headed for the lodge to watch the movie together.

Diary, I'm so happy my plan worked! Brooke and

I are friends and she and Max make a great couple.
Too bad camp is almost over.

Dear Diary,
    I wish camp weren't ending already!
Tomorrow is our last day. We leave in
the morning.

    Tonight was the perfect ending for camp, though.
We had a special campfire under a full moon.
    Nancy stood up and gave out small wooden
Evergreen trees to everyone.
"This has been a wonderful
summer," she said. "I'm so
proud of everyone. You all
worked so hard. And I hope
you had fun."
    We did, I thought, *I really did!*
We sang the Evergreen camp song. Then it was
time for the younger kids to head to bed.
    Rick and another counsellor stood up. "Let's all
say goodbye to the older Evergreeners," Rick said.
    Instantly the whole cabin of Toadstool boys
rushed up to me. "Bye, Mary-Kate!" Ethan said.
"Don't forget to eat lots of worms!"
    "Bye, worm-breath!" Ben said.
    The boys swarmed around and gave me a
group hug.

"Hey! Let me in!" a voice said. It was Jessie. She elbowed her way into the circle and joined the hug.

"I'll miss you guys!" I said. "But guess what? I'll be coming back as a junior counsellor next summer! So maybe I'll see you then."

"You'd better learn to eat beetles by then," Mojo warned me.

I laughed as Rick and John led them off to bed. Then I gave Jessie one last hug. "Thanks for being my Little Sister," I told her.

"You're the best Big Sister I ever had," she said.

When she was gone, Jill approached the Tree Frogs. "I have one last surprise for you," she said to us. "Follow me."

Where to? I wondered.

Jill led us to the big sign at the entrance to Camp Evergreen.

"See the back of this sign?" She shone her flashlight on the wooden support posts. They were all covered with carved initials and names.

I never noticed that before, Diary. Who looks at the *back* of a sign?

"Those are all the names of kids who helped win the secret challenge over the years," Jill said. "It's a tradition. If you helped get the portrait, you carve your name here."

"Cool!" I said. "But what about the guys?"

Jill shone her light down the path. Patrick, Jason, Max, Andrew and a few other boys were trudging towards us.

"They're coming," Jill said. She handed me her pocketknife and I went first. Then all my friends took turns.

While Ashley and Brooke were waiting their turn, I saw them give each other their e-mail addresses and phone numbers. Who knows? Maybe they'll even see each other during the school year, somehow.

Patrick was the last one from our team to carve his name. When he had finished, he turned to me and said, "Guess what?"

"What?" I asked.

"Nancy said I got the job. I'm going to be a C.I.T. next year, too," he said.

"Seriously?" I asked. That was great news!

So here I am, Diary, writing my last entry at camp for the summer. But all I can say is – I can hardly wait to come back next year!

PSST! Take a sneak peek
at

TWO of a kind™ Diaries 34

Dare To Scare

Dear Diary,

My cousin Jeremy and I peeked inside the dining hall. Ashley and our friends were there. So were Miranda Hong and the Hair-raiser committee from Warwick House.

"Perfect," I whispered. All I had to do was scare someone in front of the Warwick girls and I'd get to be part of their Haunted Hair-raiser House. And part of the coolest group on campus.

But then I saw Mrs. Pritchard at the teachers' table. "I can't do this!" I shut the door. "Not with the head-mistress watching!"

"Who says you can't?" Jeremy asked. "When the Head sees you, she'll know she picked the right girl for the job."

Maybe Jeremy was right – for a change. "Okay," I said, adjusting the gory costume I was wearing. "I'll do it."

Jeremy opened the door and shoved me inside.

"Owwww!" I cried as I staggered through the dining

hall. "Has anyone seen the school nurse?" I stumbled between tables. I clawed at kids with my phony scarred hands. Soon I was standing at the teachers' table – right behind Mrs. Pritchard.

"Oh, my!" Mrs. Pritchard said.

I was about to lean over the Head's shoulder when I felt a tiny twitch under my rubber eyeball. Then the bulgy rubber eye popped right off. It landed with a splat in Mrs. Pritchard's bowl of oatmeal!

The dining hall was silent as Mrs. Pritchard spooned the eyeball out of her oatmeal.

Then I heard a giggle. And another. And another. Soon everyone in the dining hall was hysterical.

Everyone except Miranda.

"That was funny, Mary-Kate!" Mrs. Pritchard said. "Well done!"

Wait! I wasn't supposed to be funny. I was supposed to be gross. Repulsive. Terrifying. Anything but funny!

How am I ever going to get a part in the Hair-raiser House now?

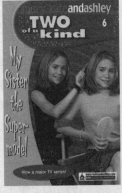

mary-kateandashley

TWO of a kind ™

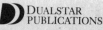

HarperCollins*Entertainment*

PARACHUTE PRESS

DUALSTAR PUBLICATIONS

AOL mary-kateandashley.com
AOL Keyword: mary-kateandashley

TM & © 2002 Dualstar Entertainment Group, LLC.

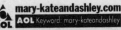

the **mary-kate**and**ashley** brand

Fab freebie!

You can have loads of fun with this ultra-cool Glistening Stix from the **mary-kate**and**ashley** brand.
Great glam looks for eyes, lips – or anywhere else you fancy!

All you have to do is **collect four tokens from four different books from the mary-kateandashley** brand
(no photocopies, please!), send them to us with your address
on the coupon below – and a groovy Glistening Stix will be on its way to you!

Go on, get collecting and sparkle like a star!

Real Books for Real Girls

It's
What
YOU
Read
